TRUCK
Donald Crews

THE BODLEY HEAD   London Sydney Toronto

First published by Greenwillow Books, New York, 1980
First published in Great Britain, 1981

British Library Cataloguing in Publication Data
Crews, Donald. Truck. 1. Title
629.22'4 TL 230   ISBN 0–370–30396–2
The art was prepared in four halftone separations
combined with black line drawings.
To A/N/A/D/J/M and especially Malcolm

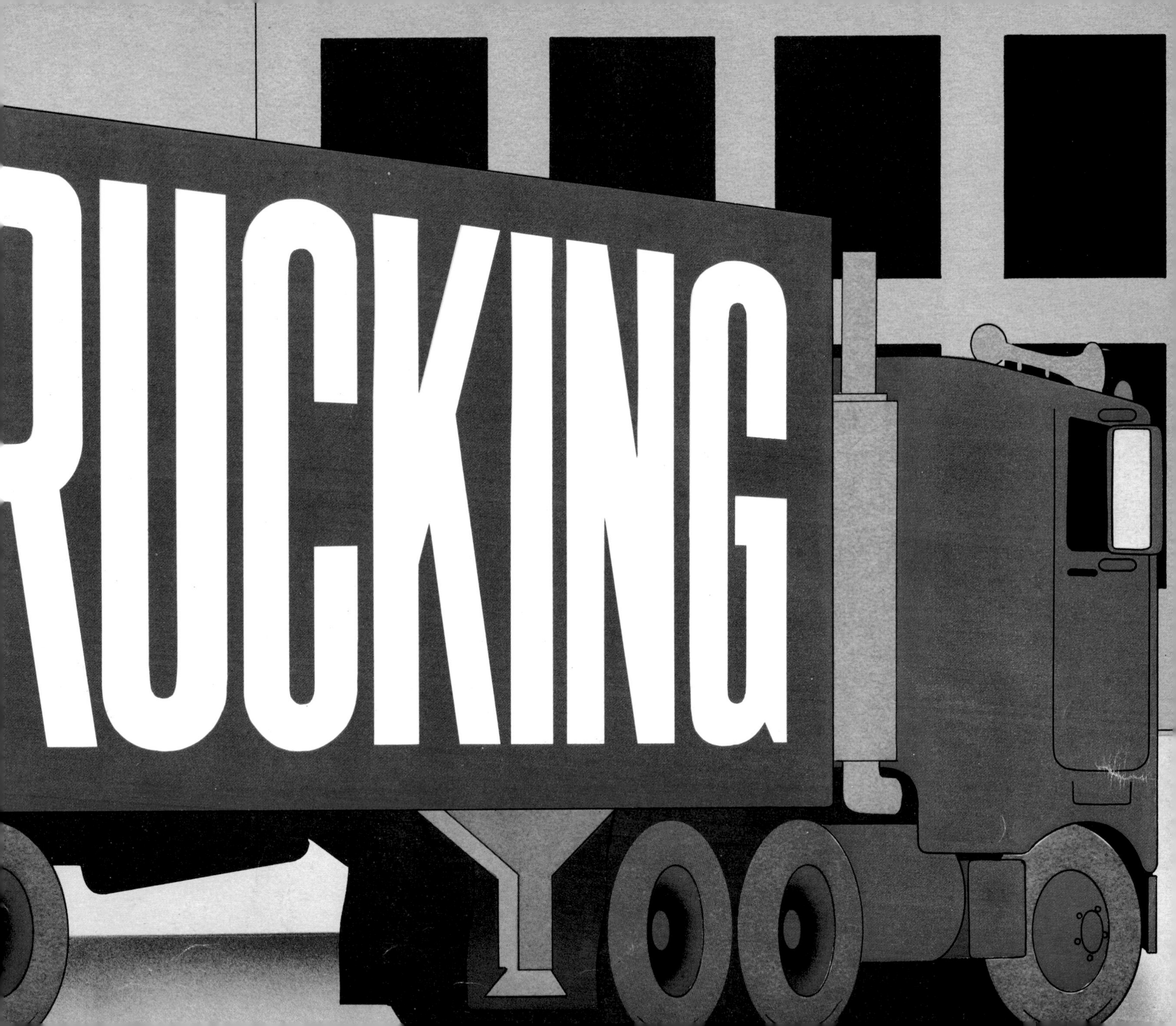
RUCKING

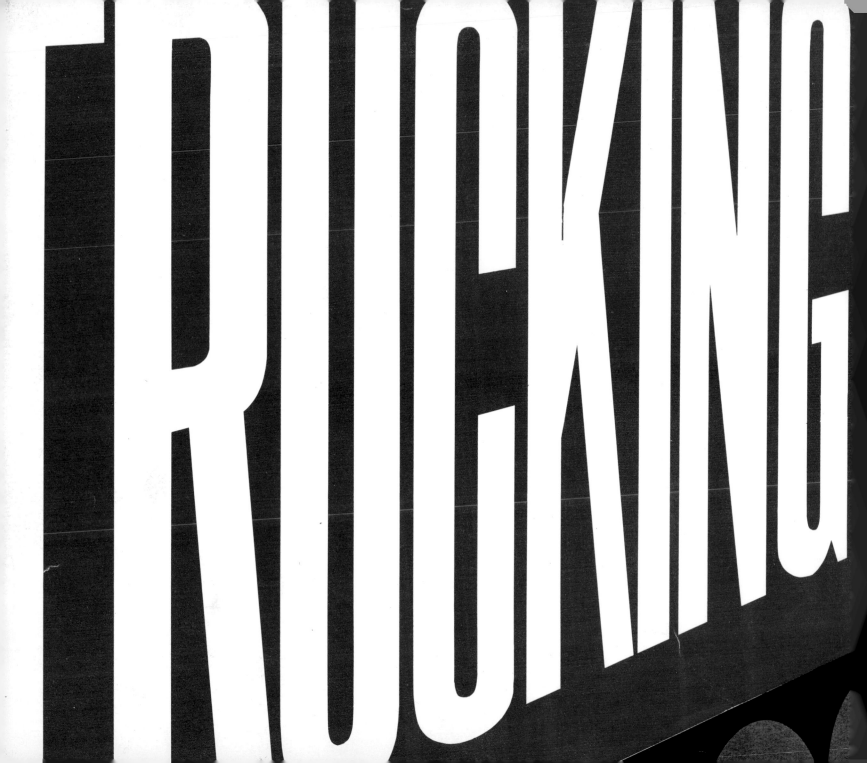

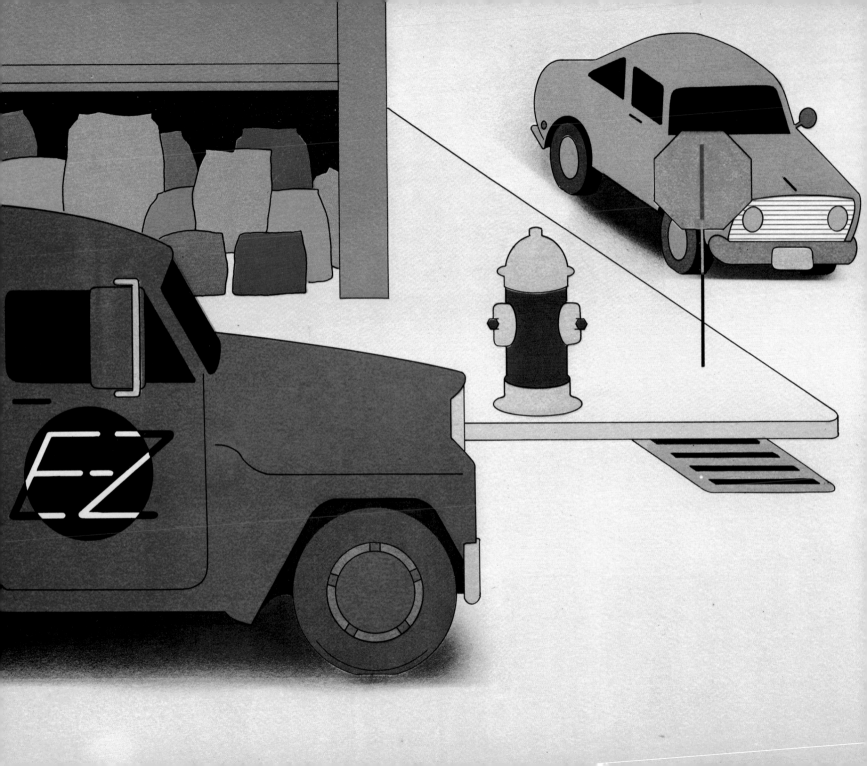

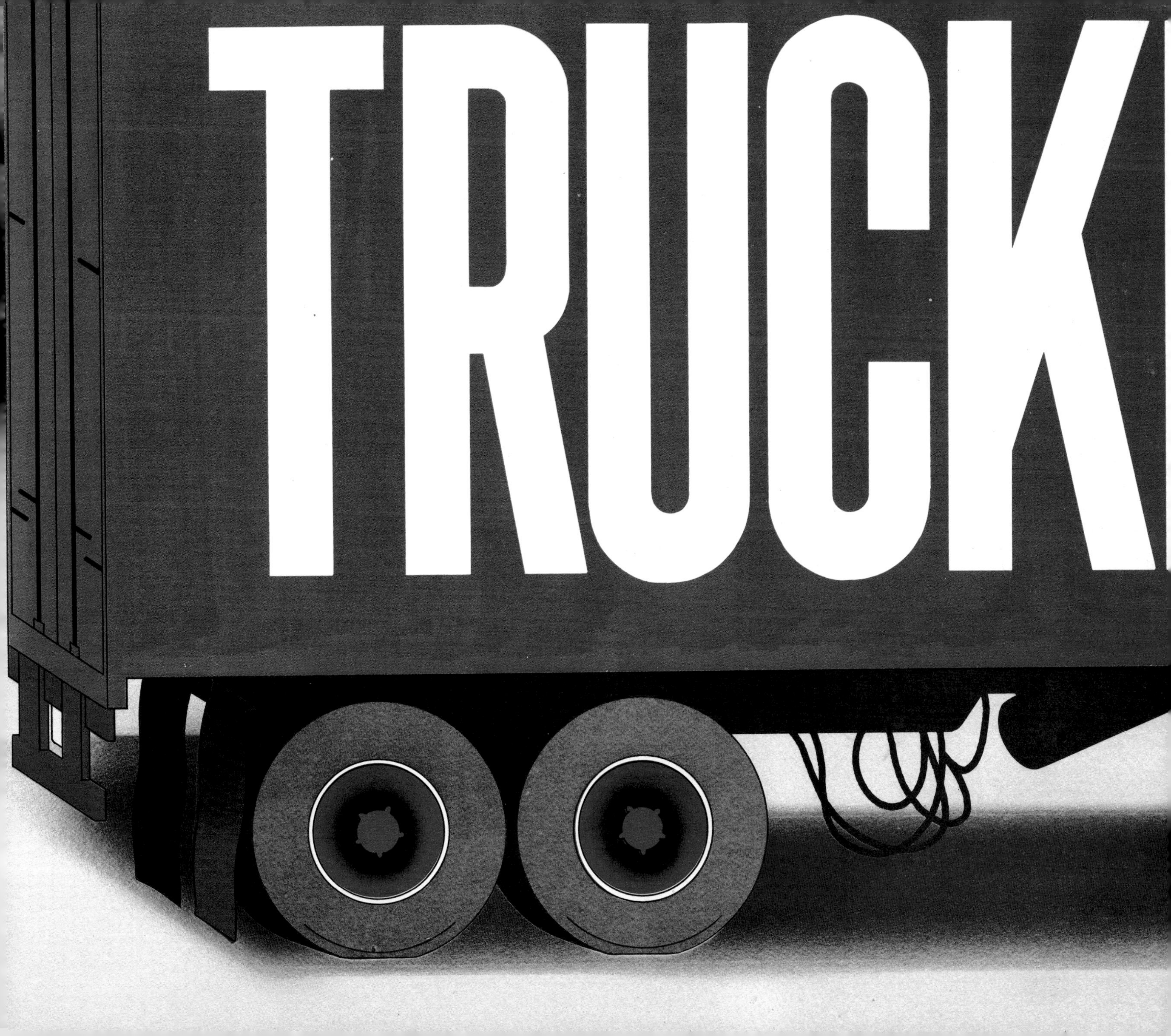
TRUCK

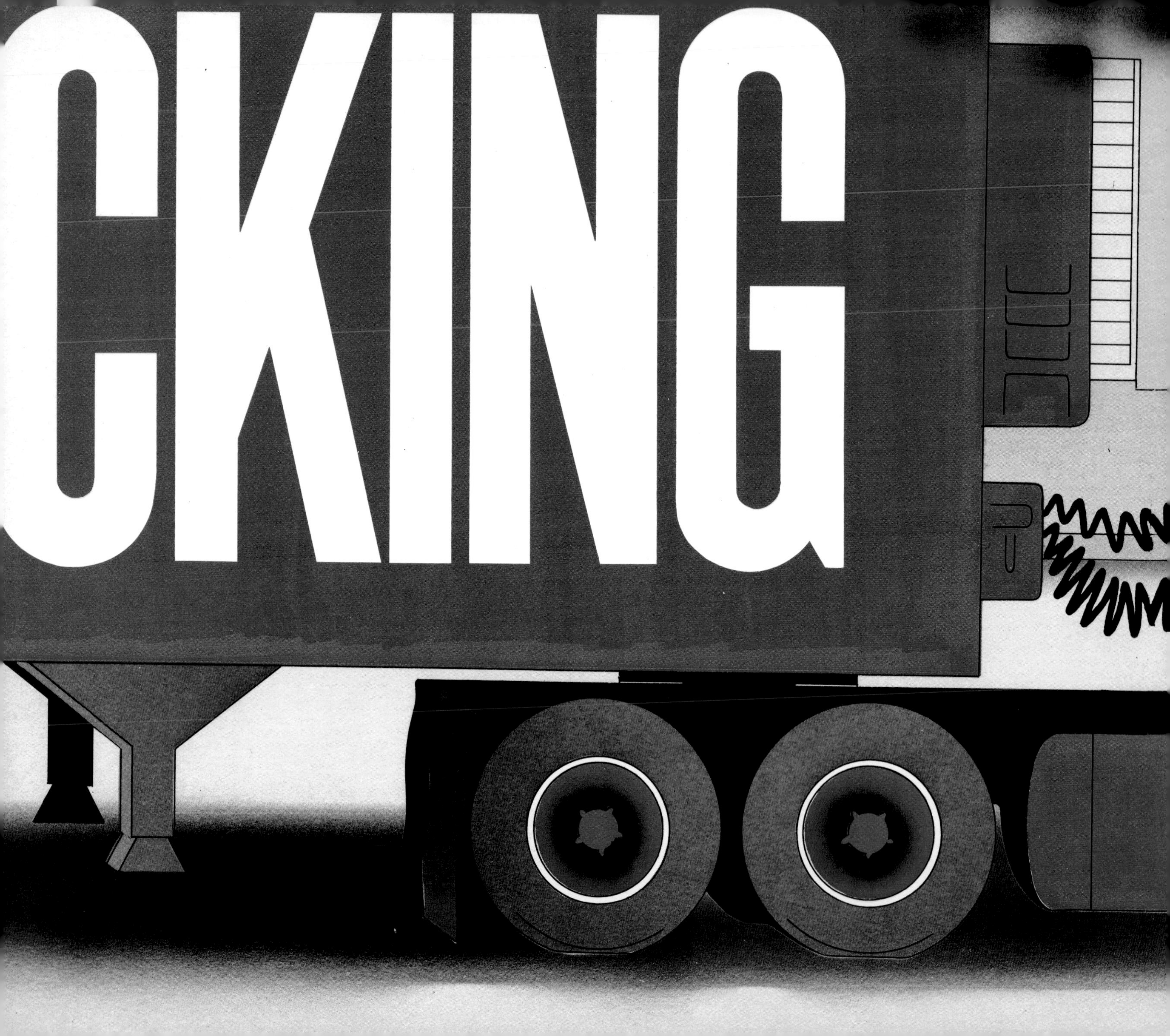
CKING

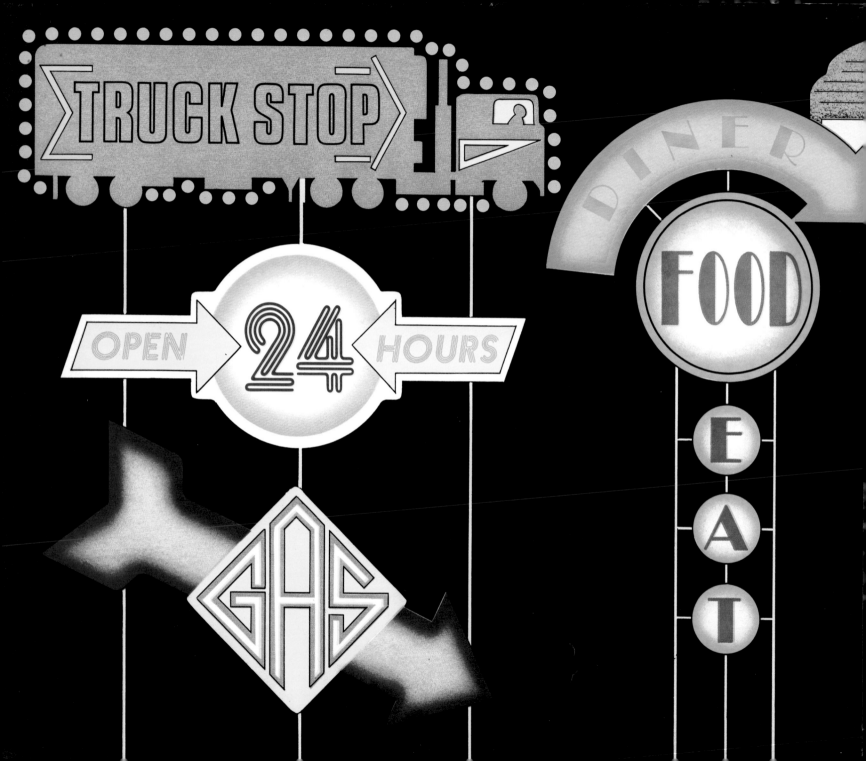

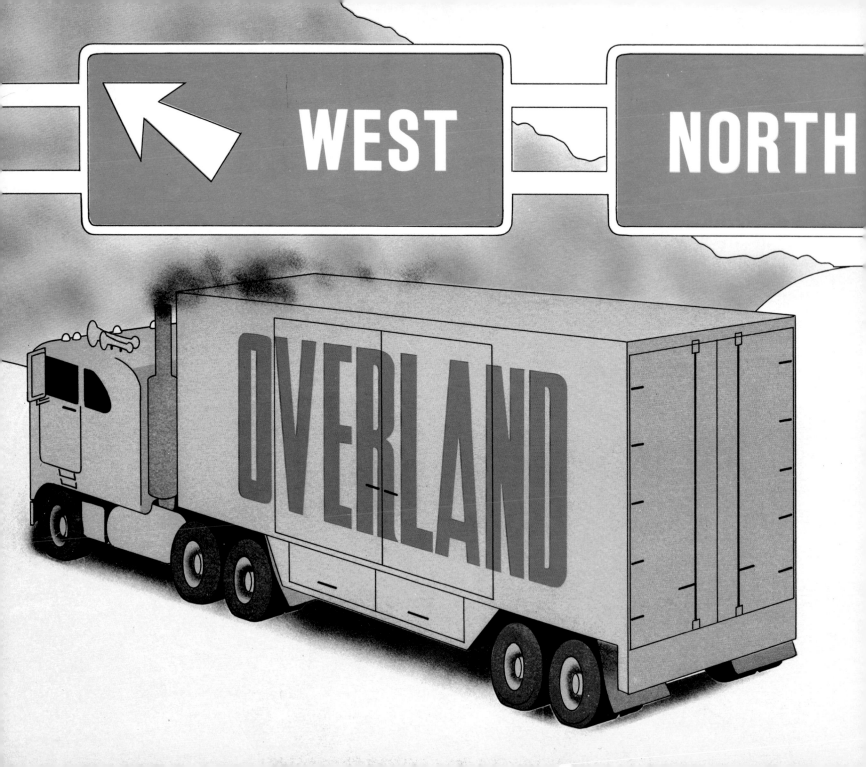